W9-AJP-110

SPOILED ROTTEN

SPOILED ROTTEN

BARTHE DeCLEMENTS

Illustrated by JENNIFER PLECAS

Hyperion Books for Children
New York

For information address Hyperion Books for Children, 114 Fifth Avenue, New York, New York 10011-5690.

Printed in the United States of America.

3 5 7 9 10 8 6 4 2

The artwork for each picture is prepared using watercolor.
This book is set in 18-point Berkeley Book.

Library of Congress Cataloging-in-Publication Data
DeClements, Barthe.
Spoiled rotten / Barthe DeClements ; illustrated by Jennifer Plecas.
p. cm.
Summary: Scott helps his best friend Andy learn how to follow the rules in second grade so that he will not get in trouble.
ISBN 0-7868-1145-5 (pbk.)—ISBN 0-7868-2317-8 (lib. bdg.)
[1. Behavior—Fiction. 2. Schools—Fiction. 3. Friendship—Fiction.] I. Plecas, Jennifer, ill. II. Title.
PZ7.D3584Sp 1996
[Fic]—dc20 95-51097

This book is dedicated to my delightful granddaughter, Katya.

—B. D.

I would like to thank Deborah Halverson, Jennifer Cobb, Kristin Galanti, and the students for sharing their school experiences with me. I would also like to express my indebtedness to Susan Brown and Jacqueline Hallquist for their invaluable input on the manuscript.

Contents

1
Foxy Brown

Andy's mom pushed open his bedroom door. "I thought you boys might like a snack."

"Sure," Andy said and grabbed for the food.

His mom yanked the tray back. "Guests

are first, sweetie."

She gave me a jelly donut and pop. Then she gave some to Andy and took the tray away.

We sat on his bed with the pop cans between our knees.

"Mmm. Good," I said when I took a bite of the squishy donut.

"Better than the apples we get at your house," Andy said.

"You're the only kid here. There are four kids at my house. My mom says she can't waste money on junk food."

Andy made his mad face. "This isn't junk, Scott."

"It'll rot your teeth."

When his face got madder, I threw my empty pop can in the wastebasket. "Hey, let's play your baseball game."

Andy pulled his plastic bat and ball

out of his closet. I took out the shooter. The shooter has a spring on the inside and a pedal on the outside. You put the ball on the spring, step on the pedal, and the ball flies up.

We dragged the stuff into Andy's backyard. Before he took a turn, he yelled, "Mom, Mom! Come see me bat."

She came running onto the porch.

He stepped on the pedal, the ball flew up, and he swung the bat. And missed. He missed the next time, too.

"Good try!" she called and went in the house.

"Wait, Mom!" he yelled. "I have another turn."

She came running out again.

This time he ticked the ball with the bat. It dribbled across the grass to me.

"Andy, you hit it! That's very good. I'm

sure you'll do great in second grade," she said and went inside.

Andy missed the next ball. He handed me the bat without a squawk.

I hit my first ball about three yards. Andy tossed it back to me. I hit the second one at least ten yards. Andy had to run for it.

I missed the third ball. But the fourth one landed in the alley. Andy came puffing back with it.

"Scott, I know what we should do," he said, holding on to the ball. "We should play a new game. In this one you only get three hits, but as many strikes as you want."

"No way!" I said. "You know it's three strikes and you're out."

"Yes, but this is a new game," Andy said. "You can have maybe ten strikes in this game. But you have to give up the ball after three hits."

"No, you don't," I told him. "It's three strikes and you're out."

"No, it's my bat and ball. I get to say the game we play."

"And you get to play by yourself, too." I dropped the bat and marched through his gate and into my yard.

"Hey," he called after me. "We've got more donuts."

I kept marching to my back door. I wasn't playing his stupid game. Not even for a jelly donut.

Mom and my big sister, Pat, were in the kitchen making dinner. "You didn't stay at Andy's very long," Mom said.

"That's because he cheats. He changes the rules so he can win."

Pat was peeling carrots at the sink. "Andy's spoiled rotten," she said.

"Well," Mom said, "he'll learn to share in regular school."

My brother, Jay, came in and grabbed a peeled carrot. "When who is in regular school?"

"Andy. He's going into the second grade with Scott tomorrow," Mom said.

"Only for a tryout," I said. "Andy just turned seven this week. The principal said Andy could *try* second grade to see how he gets along."

Jay poked me with his carrot. "You guys are lucky. The second-grade teacher is Ms. Brown. She's a fox."

"Too foxy for you," Pat said to Jay. "Ms. Brown was on to all your tricks."

"No way," he said.

Pat laughed at him. "You spent half your recesses with your head on your desk."

"I'm not going to do anything bad," I said. "I'm not going to lose my recess."

"Your friend Andy can't follow rule one," Pat said. "He won't last a week in second grade. Then he'll have to go in first grade."

Andy had never been in first grade. His

family had stayed in motels while his house was being built next to ours. His mom said it would be better for her to teach him than to have him hop from school to school.

I wasn't so sure about that.

2
You Look like a Nerd

Everyone in our house rushed around the next morning. Except Dad. He told me to knock 'em dead and went off to work.

I took too long in the bathroom. Jay came in and shoved me away from the sink.

"You're pretty enough," he said.

I walked up and down the hall, waiting for Pat. I needed her to check me over. I didn't want to look dumb in second grade.

Pat came out of her bedroom.

I asked her, "Am I all right?"

I had on my new jeans and Save the Whales T-shirt. The T-shirt was her idea. She said Ms. Brown would like it.

"Your clothes are okay," Pat said. "But what did you do to your hair?"

"I wet it down so it would stay flat."

"Too nerdy. Go get my blow-dryer and a comb."

She blow-dried my hair and combed it into place. I stood in front of the hall

mirror after she was done. I did look better.

It's five blocks to the grade school. Mom pushed Caroline in her stroller.

I saw Kenny across the street with his Seahawks cap on the back of his head. He was walking by himself. His mom probably had to work.

"I wish I had a cap like Kenny's," I told my mom.

"I thought you were going to die unless you got the running shoes you're wearing," Mom said.

"Well, I needed these, too." I stopped to tie my shoelaces again. I didn't catch up with Mom until we reached Ms. Brown's classroom.

Ms. Brown had on green glass earrings. She smiled at me. "I'm glad you're going to be in my class, Scott."

"I think he'll be easier on you than Jay was," Mom told her.

Ms. Brown laughed.

Andy and his mom came into the classroom next.

While Ms. Brown talked to them, Mom helped me find the desk with my name tag on it. Three other desks were pushed against it. Together, they made one big desk with four chairs.

Before Mom left, she said to me, "Now, don't try to 'knock 'em dead.' Just behave yourself."

I promised I would.

Andy's name was on the desk across from mine. "Hey, Andy," I called. "You sit in my group."

Andy and his mom came over to his seat.

He stuck his giant box of crayons in

his desk. Then he stuck in his box of colored pencils, his glue, and his scissors. Then he stuck in his head to see if everything was in the right place.

The only thing left on his desk was his ratty bear.

Ms. Brown said, "We'll let Mom take this home with her." She handed the stuffed bear to Andy's mom.

I thought maybe he'd grab it back. He didn't. He just watched his mom and his bear go out the door.

After all the kids found their seats, Ms. Brown wrote her name on the board. She told us she lived with four cats. They were named Princess, King, Duke, and Merlin the Magician. The one named Merlin was always disappearing.

She said each of us should tell the class about ourselves. She called on Kenny first. He was sitting with his hands folded. He still had on his Seahawks cap.

Kenny said, “I live with my mom and my aunt Judy. We have a dog named Bruce. He’s a Doberman pinscher. He bited two times. If he does it again, he has to be put to sleep.”

“Oh, my,” Ms. Brown said. “I hope you have a strong fence.”

“Our fence is six feet. But Bruce bited the UPS man,” Kenny explained.

“Oh, my,” Ms. Brown said again. “Thank you, Kenny. Jill, you’re sitting up tall. Will you share with us?”

Jill was in the chair beside me. I didn’t know her.

She said there were six kids in her family. She was the oldest. She had to change the baby’s diapers every day.

Yuck!

Andy jumped up. "I'll be next. I have a ten-speed bike and a computer and . . ."

"Just a minute, Andy," Ms. Brown said. "In second grade we wait until we're called upon. Class, what other school rules can we share with Andy?"

I raised my hand, but Ms. Brown

called on Martha.

Martha took in a long breath before she started. "Don't run in the classroom. Don't talk out loud when the teacher's talking. Raise your hand. Umm . . . umm . . . Use an inside voice. Don't talk back. Umm . . . umm . . . Don't climb on your desk. Umm . . ."

She was using up all the rules!

"Outstanding, Martha," Ms. Brown said. "Seth, can you think of another rule?"

"No," Seth said.

"Let's look at this poster on the wall." Ms. Brown pointed to the poster.

It had four rules written on top. Below the rules were pockets with our names on them. Cards were stuck in the pockets.

The first card had a gold star on it. The

cards behind it were different colors.

Ms. Brown read the rules. "One: keep your hands, feet, and objects to yourself. Two: <u>no</u> swearing or teasing. Three: follow directions the first time. Four: raise your hand if you wish to speak."

Ms. Brown took a yellow card out of a pocket. "If you forget a rule, you put the yellow card in front of your star. That's a warning. If you forget again, the blue card goes in front and you lose five minutes of your recess."

I looked at Andy. He was cutting off the corners of his name tag.

"I want all eyes over here," Ms. Brown said. "You too, Andy."

Andy sneaked his scissors into his desk.

Ms. Brown told us that if we got the purple card in front we had to spend a whole recess with our head down. And if the red card was in front, we had to call home.

Ms. Brown went to the shelves beside her desk. She lifted off a cardboard box. "This is the treasure box. Inside are cars, stickers, squirt guns, whistles, magic notes, pom-poms."

When she held up the pom-poms, Jill went, "Ohh."

I didn't. I wanted the little orange car.

Ms. Brown gave us a big smile. "On Fridays, we'll check the cards. If a star is in front of your name, you go to the treasure box. You can pick out anything you want. To keep."

She put the treasure box away.

We finished telling about ourselves before we went home. Andy spent his turn telling about all his games.

When my turn came, I said, "I have one brother. He's in sixth grade. I have a big sister in junior high. And I have a baby sister. But I don't have to change her stinky diapers."

3
The Big Rats

On Tuesday, Ms. Brown gave each group a maple leaf. "Place it in the center of your desks," she said. "That way everyone can see it."

Jill put our leaf in the middle of our desks.

Next, Ms. Brown passed out sheets of white paper. "I thought it would look pretty to have colored leaves on our windows. You can draw a maple leaf on your paper. And color it any way you like."

I took my crayons out of my desk. But before I could see how to draw the leaf, Andy snatched it.

"Put that back," Jill said to him. "It's supposed to stay in the middle of our desks."

"Just a minute. I have to make my outline first." Andy stuck the leaf on his white paper and started to draw around it.

Sarah sat next to me. She stared at Andy until her face got red. "You put that back! It's not yours."

Andy went right on drawing.

Sarah grabbed for the leaf. Andy plopped his hand over it. Sarah scratched at his hand.

Andy yelled, "Cut that out!"

Ms. Brown hurried to our group. "What seems to be the problem?"

"Andy took the maple leaf," Jill explained.

"Andy," Ms. Brown said, "we are in groups in second grade so we can help one another."

"I'm going to give the leaf back as soon

as I'm done," he mumbled.

Ms. Brown pointed Andy's chin at the poster. "Read rule three."

"'Follow directions the first time.'"

"And what were the directions?" she asked.

"'Place the leaf in the center of the desks.'" He pushed it off his paper.

She gave his shoulder a pat and went over to Kenny's group.

Nobody talked in our group while we were drawing and cutting.

My leaf was red and orange. Jill and Sarah's leaves were yellow and green. Andy's was all red.

He called, "Ms. Brown, Ms. Brown! See mine."

She was busy with Martha's group.

Andy jumped out of his chair. He went across the room, carrying his leaf.

"Andy," Ms. Brown asked, "why are you out of your seat?"

"Don't you want to see my leaf?" He held it under her nose.

She turned him around and gave him a little push. "I'll see your work when I get to your desk."

Andy put on his mad face and stamped

back to his seat.

When I got home, I told my mom how Andy acted in school.

"Well," Mom said, "he's used to getting all the attention at home. When you're in a big family, maybe you don't get as much attention. But you learn to share and be quiet some of the time."

"Ya, because if you don't, your brother slugs you," I said.

The next morning, when we got to school, maple leaves were pasted all over our windows. They looked like they were falling out of the sky.

Ms. Brown said we were going to study North American animals. She thought we might like to name our groups after animals. She took us to the library to read about them.

I thought red foxes were neat. Andy

liked black bears.

When we got back to our room, Ms. Brown said each group should decide on an animal. If we had trouble deciding, we could vote.

We had trouble deciding. Sarah and Jill wanted to name our group the Opossums.

"No. They look like big rats," Andy

said. "I saw one squashed on the road."

"Bears are fat," Sarah said. "Opossums are cute. I've got a book called *Possum Magic*. And the possums are real cute."

"They are not," Andy said. "Opossums have teeth like sharks, and rat tails."

"We'll vote," Jill said. "You first, Scott."

"Red fox," I said.

Sarah was next. She said, "Opossum."

Andy said, "Black bear!" real loud.

Jill said, "I vote for the opossum, too. So it wins."

Andy pushed his chair back and yelled, "I'm not going to be a rat!"

Ms. Brown hurried to our group. "Andy, we talk with an inside voice in the classroom. Please go put a yellow card in front of your star. That will help you remember."

Andy stamped up to the poster. He yanked the yellow card out of the pocket and stuck it in front of his star. Then he stamped back to his seat.

"Andy," Ms. Brown said. "Go put the blue card in front. You need to remember to walk like a second grader."

Andy made his mad face. Ms. Brown waited. He walked slowly to the poster and put his blue card in front of the yellow one.

After Ms. Brown left, I whispered, "Now you lose five minutes of your recess."

"I know!" he said.

We had spelling next. Six new words. Andy already knew them. His mom had taught them to him.

After spelling, Ms. Brown called the groups to go out for recess. "The Coyotes are sitting tall."

That was Kenny's group. He had his Seahawks cap on backward. I wished I had a cap.

"Bobcats," Ms. Brown called. Jim was a Bobcat. He had a yellow card. He kept tipping back his chair.

The Raccoons and Otters were next. And the White-Tailed Deer. The Opossums were last because Sarah was poky clearing off her desk.

Andy was the only one left in the room.

On the way home from school, he said, "Regular school stinks."

Pat and her boyfriend, Tim, were at my house.

"Andy thinks regular school stinks," I told them. "He lost five minutes of his recess."

"I knew he wouldn't last a week," Pat said.

I felt a little bad about that. Andy was seven months younger than I was, but two inches taller. He'd look dumb in first grade.

I noticed Tim was wearing a Mariners baseball cap. It was blue with a teal blue bill. The cap had an *S* with a compass

on it. The *S* was for Seattle.

"That's a neat cap," I told him.

He took it off and tossed it to me. "Here. You can have it."

"Are you sure?"

"Take it," Pat said. "He's got two of them."

"Wow. Thanks, Tim." I put the cap on backward and went down the hall to look in the mirror. Cool! Really cool.

4
Keep Away

"Cool cap," Andy said on our walk to school the next morning. "Where'd you get it?"

"Pat's boyfriend gave it to me."

"Ask him where he bought it so I can get one," Andy told me. "Mom's going to buy me something if I stay in second grade."

"Then you better learn the rules or you won't," I warned him.

He kicked a pop can on the sidewalk. "Ms. Brown hates me."

"No, she doesn't. You just can't pig everything," I said.

Andy kicked the can some more. "I'm not the only bad one. Jim keeps tipping back his chair."

Andy was right about that. Ms. Brown told Jim again that morning to keep all the chair's legs on the floor. "Four on the floor," she reminded him.

When Andy saw Jim tip back, he said, "Ms. Brown, Ms. Brown."

Ms. Brown was writing on the board.

"Ms. Brown!" Andy yelled.

Sarah poked him. "You have to wait until she calls on you."

"You aren't my boss," he told her. "Ms. Brown! Jim's tipping his chair back."

Ms. Brown said, "Andy, you'll have to put your purple card behind your name. You need to remember to raise your hand."

Andy stared at her with round eyes.

Ms. Brown nodded her head at the poster.

Andy walked slowly to the poster. He took the purple card out of the pocket and put it in front of the blue one.

Wow. Now he had lost his recess. And his next card was the red one. I was glad I wasn't Andy.

On the way home from school, two fifth-grade boys stopped Andy and me.

"Where'd you get that Mariners cap?" the fat one asked.

I opened my mouth to tell him, but he yanked the cap off my head.

"You give that back!" I said.

"No," he laughed. "It's too big for you."

I tried to grab the cap from him. He threw it to the skinny boy. I raced over to him. He threw it back to the fat boy. I raced to the fat boy. He waved it in the air so high I couldn't reach it. Even when I jumped.

"Give me my cap!" I yelled.

"Give it back," Andy yelled.

"Naw. It's mine now." The fat boy put it on his head.

I pulled at his hair. He shoved me so hard I fell down.

Andy rushed up and kicked him. The boy swatted at Andy. Andy ducked and

kicked him again.

The skinny boy grabbed Andy's arm. "Knock it off, you little creep."

I thought my cap was a goner. And then I saw Jay and his friend Robert coming up the street.

"Hey, what's going on?" Jay called out. "That's my brother. You guys want to get pounded?"

The skinny boy dropped Andy's arm. The fat one took my cap off his head. He threw it at my face.

"We were just playing with them," he said when Jay reached us.

I stood up. "No, he wasn't, Jay. He stole my cap."

"We were just kidding around, honest," the skinny one said. He jerked his head at the fat boy. "Let's take off."

They did. They both ran as fast as they could.

Jay grinned at Andy. "You sure jumped into that scrap."

"I had to," Andy said. "Scott's my friend."

5
Sad Andy

"Ms. Brown hates me," Andy told all the kids at lunch the next day.

"No, she doesn't," Jill said. "She doesn't hate kids."

"Then why didn't she make Jim change his card?" Andy wanted to know. "He tipped back his chair."

"But you yelled out first," Jill said. "You should learn to keep your mouth shut."

"You'd know how if you had a big brother," I said.

"Kenny doesn't have any brothers or sisters," Kate said, "and he doesn't get in trouble."

"Ms. Brown probably likes Kenny," Andy said.

Each afternoon Ms. Brown read to us

before we went home. But first we had to pick the junk off the floor and clear our desks. Andy likes stories and he was ready first.

He sat up straight. I did, too. And so did Jill.

Sarah was poky clearing her desk.

"The White-Tailed Deer are ready for a story," Ms. Brown said. "And the Otters' floor looks super clean."

"Hurry up," Andy whispered to Sarah.

She made a face at him instead of putting her crayons away. He reached over and scooped them into her lap. One of them fell on the floor and broke.

"Dumb *boy*! See what you did!" She punched him in the arm.

Ms. Brown said, "Sarah. Andy. Change your cards, please."

Sarah went to the poster and put a

blue card behind her name.

Andy just sat there. He looked like he'd been smacked in the head with a soccer ball.

"Andy," Ms. Brown said, "read rule one."

Andy read in a little voice. "'Keep your hands, feet, and objects to yourself.'"

He pulled himself up and put the red card behind his name.

Ms. Brown took her book off her desk. She sat on a chair in front of the room. All the kids sat on the floor around her.

Except Andy. He sat slumped against the wall. He wouldn't look at anyone. He was all alone with his head hung over his crossed legs.

When Ms. Brown was halfway through the story, I peeked at him again. He looked so sad I was afraid he'd cry.

I slid sideways until I was in front of him. Then if he cried, none of the kids could see him.

Mom was feeding Caroline when I got home.

"Andy got the red card today," I told her. "He had to call his mom."

"What did his mother do?" Mom asked.

"I don't know. He stayed after school. Ms. Brown had to take him to the office phone."

I leaned on Mom's chair and patted Caroline on her bald head. "Did Jay ever have to call you?"

"No, thank goodness. Go get me a clean diaper."

"And then can I go over to Andy's?"

"Maybe he won't feel like having company."

"Sure he will. He likes company."

I found Andy sitting on his back porch. He was slumped down again. And he looked like he'd been crying.

I sat beside him. "What happened?"

"I had to tell my mom what I did in school."

"What did she say?" I asked.

"She said to try harder. But Ms. Brown

said maybe I'd be happier in first grade. She said that's where you learn to follow directions. She said I was a smart boy. And she bet I'd catch on fast in first grade."

"If you're so smart," I said, "why can't you catch on in second grade?"

"I don't know," he mumbled.

"Do you have to go in first grade tomorrow?" I asked him.

"No. My mom got Ms. Brown to give me another week to prove myself."

"That's really good," I said. "Ms. Brown puts all the gold stars back on Monday. You can keep yours next week."

"I'll never make it," Andy said sadly. Tears rolled down his cheeks.

"I'll help you," I said.

Andy just shook his head. And more tears rolled down his face.

We sat down on the steps. I sighed. Andy sighed.

"I've got it! I've got it!" I yelled. "The Mariners pitcher pulls on his cap to signal the catcher. I've seen him on TV. You watch my cap. And I'll pull on it when your star's in danger."

Andy shook his head. "I can't watch

your cap all day."

"Sure you can. You can keep one eye on it. You can use your other eye to do your work.

"Listen," I said. "Tomorrow is Friday. You already have the red card so you can't get any worse. You just have to keep your mouth shut and your hands to yourself. We'll practice tomorrow, okay?"

"Okay," he agreed. But I think he was so sad he didn't really care.

6
Frog Mouth

The next day I was so busy pulling on my cap I could hardly do my work.

Ms. Brown passed out baskets of tiny cubes for math. Andy took two handfuls.

I pulled and pulled on my cap. Then I coughed.

Andy put one handful back in the basket.

Sarah said, "What's happened to you, Piggy?" But Ms. Brown didn't hear her.

Before we went home, six kids got to go to the treasure box. Kenny was first. I hoped and hoped he wouldn't choose the orange car. He didn't. He took a sheet of stickers to his seat.

Jill was next. She couldn't decide

between a pom-pom and stickers. Ms. Brown reminded her that other students were waiting their turns.

"I know. I know," Jill said, jiggling up and down. "But I want them both."

She dropped the stickers back in the box and kept the pom-pom.

And it was my turn. Finally!

It took me one second to pick out the orange car. I rolled it around my desk while the last three kids went to the treasure box.

I rolled it up the sidewalk when Andy and I walked home.

"Isn't it neat?" I asked him.

"It's okay," he said.

"There's a blue car in the box. You can get that next week."

"I probably won't get anything," Andy said.

"Sure you will. Just keep watching my cap. Then you'll go to the treasure box."

I know he didn't believe me.

But he tried really hard on Monday anyway. He was so quiet and smart, he got a smiley face on his spelling paper.

He kept his star on Tuesday when we wrote stories about our groups' animals.

And he tried even harder to keep his star on Wednesday. We made pictures to go with our stories.

Andy put a long tail on his opossum. He made the tail wind all round the corners of his paper.

"Opossum tails aren't *that* long," Sarah told him.

"Yes, they are," Andy said. "Opossums are big rats."

Jill was looking through her crayon box. "Oh, I don't have any gray," she cried.

Andy shoved his giant box toward her desk. "Here, I've got three grays."

Jill took one out of his box.

"Good for you, Andy," Ms. Brown said. "That's how we help each other."

Andy sneaked me a little smile. I sneaked a smile back.

Thursday morning, I noticed Sarah's

face looked funny. She had something in her mouth that flopped up and down.

"What have you got in your mouth?" I asked her.

"It's a spacer so my teeth come in straight," she said.

"You look like a frog," I said.

"Croak! Croak!" Andy said.

We didn't see Ms. Brown beside us.

Sarah did. "Ms. Brown, Scott said I look like a frog. And Andy went, 'Croak, croak.'"

"I know," Ms. Brown said. "Scott. Andy. Do we tease in second grade?"

"No," we mumbled.

"Put your yellow cards in front of your stars," Ms. Brown told us.

On our way home, Andy said, "I knew I'd never make it."

"Ms. Brown will still let you stay in second grade," I said. "You just can't go to the treasure box."

"How do you know?" Andy asked.

"Because yellow is only a warning," I explained. "Watch my cap so you don't get the blue card tomorrow."

Andy tried hard again. He didn't make a

peep on Friday. Not a peep all day. I kept looking at Ms. Brown to see if she was noticing.

At three o'clock, she said, "We have ten people to go to the treasure box."

Kenny took a whistle. Jill took stickers. And even Sarah got to get a pom-pom.

It wasn't fair. Andy had tried and tried to be good. Sarah was a little tattletale. If I hadn't called her a frog, Andy would have gone to the treasure box.

I slowly pulled my library book out of my desk. Andy already had his nose in his.

"And before we go home," Ms. Brown said, "I have a special badge for the most improved student. Who do you think that is?"

All the kids pointed to Andy. His eyes got big and round.

Ms. Brown took a star to his desk and pinned it on his T-shirt.

Andy looked down at the star. And he looked up at Ms. Brown. "Will you let me stay in second grade?" he whispered.

She gave his arm a pat. "For sure. You act like a second grader to me."

Andy's mouth fell open. For a second, I thought he might fall off his chair.

But after school he went hopping down the street. "Mom will buy me a cap like yours, Scott."

"And you can get the blue car next week," I told him.

"No." He grinned. "I'm going to get the squirt gun."